Lightning Fred

First published in Great Britain 1985 by Heinemann Young Books
Paperback edition first published 1998 by Mammoth
an imprint of Egmont Children's Books Limited
239 Kensington High Street, London W8 6SA
Published in hardback by Heinemann Educational Publishing Limited
a division of Reed Educational and Professional Publishing Limited
by arrangement with Egmont Children's Books Limited
Text copyright © Dick King-Smith 1985
Illustrations copyright © Sarah Nayler 1998
The Author and Illustrator have asserted their moral rights
Paperback ISBN 0 7497 3374 8
Hardback ISBN 0 434 80294 8
10 9 8 7 6 5 4 3 2
A CIP catalogue record for this title is available from the British Library
Printed at Oriental Press Limited, Dubai

Lightning Fred

Dick King-Smith

Illustrated by *Sarah Nayler*

 **YELLOW BANANAS**

Chapter One

DIGBY WAS NINE and tubby and Dot was seven and short in the leg. They were not fast runners. This didn't bother Dot, but Digby's secret ambition had always been to win a race at the School Sports. One year, when there had been chicken-pox, he had come in third. But then there had only been two other boys running.

'Only a week to Sports Day and this year I'll be in the Boys' Under-Ten 100 metres,' thought Digby, red-faced and puffing, not from thinking it but from running back from

school to get home before the threat
of a thunderstorm.

'Quick!' their mother had
called from the cottage door as
they stumbled up the garden path,
forgetting to shut the gate, and quick,
thought Digby, is what I wish I was.

Now he knelt beside his sister on the sofa
and looked out at the rain bucketing down.

'Phoo!' he said as the lightning flashed. 'Glad

2

we're out of that.'

Dot let out a sudden wail. 'Fred!' she cried. 'Where's Fred?'

At that moment the lawn outside was suddenly lit up and thunder banged almost immediately.

'There he is,' said Digby. 'By the sundial. Hope it doesn't act as a lightning conductor.'

'Oh, Dig, don't say that! Oh, Mum, can I get him in?'

'No, certainly not,' said their mother. 'Tortoises

are quite safe in thunderstorms. He'll just pull his head and legs in and let the rain bounce off his shell,' and she went out of the room.

The next instant there came a huge clap of thunder, right above the cottage roof it seemed, and a brilliant crackling, hissing

zigzag that almost blinded them.
Automatically, they put their hands before
their eyes.

When they looked again, they could see that
the tortoise was lying tipped up on his back.
He seemed to steam slightly in the pouring rain.

Chapter Two

'HE MUST HAVE a proper grave,' sobbed Dot.

The storm had gone, and the children stood by the motionless shape of Fred. Digby had tipped him right side up with the toe of his wellie, and they could actually see where the bolt of lightning had hit him. They had painted their name and address and telephone number on his shell, but now most of the red paint had disappeared under a crescent-shaped brown scorch-mark that left only the phone number showing.

Digby bent down to touch this mark with a

finger, and then suddenly leapt very high in the air.

Dot stopped crying in amazement.

'Dig!' she said. 'I didn't know you could jump that high!'

'Nor did I,' said Digby. 'It gave me a sort of shock, touching that burn-mark. Not a nasty shock, just sort of exciting. It made me feel, well, powerful. You try it.'

'No, no. I don't want to touch him. We must bury him. Will you make a hole?'

'All right.'

'And we ought to write something. Like they have on gravestones. Can you think something up, Dig?'

Digby thought.

'How about this?' he said.

'Here lies our tortoise.

His name is Fred.

He was alive.

But now he's dead.'

'That's lovely,' said Dot in a choked voice. She blew her nose hard.

'You go and write that out on a bit of wood or something,' said Digby, 'while I get the grave ready. Under the weeping willow tree.'

A couple of minutes later, Dot came running back to the sundial, carrying her handiwork. There was no sign of Fred, so she ran to the willow tree where Digby stood beside an empty hole.

'Why didn't you bring him?' he said.

'I thought you'd fetched him,' she replied.

They stared at each other. Then they began

to grin like gargoyles.

'He wasn't dead!'

'He's walked away!'

'Good old Fred!'

'Let's tell Mum!'

They ran indoors. 'Mum! Mum, Fred's not dead!'

'Oh, good, I am glad.'

'He's wandered off somewhere. We're going to look for him.'

'I expect he's shell-shocked. Anyway, while you're looking, I'm just going to walk up to

the post-box with these letters. Shan't be
long.'

Just after she had gone, the phone rang.
Digby ran indoors to answer it. He came back
to Dot, looking thoughtful.

'Who was it, Dig?'

'A lady ringing up to say she'd found a
tortoise.'

'Who? Where?'

'Someone who lives in Hatch Norton.'
Hatch Norton was the next village.

'But that's two miles
away!'

'Yes.'

'And Fred's only been gone ten minutes.'

'Yes.'

Dot struggled to do the sum in her head.

'He must have been going at least twelve

miles an hour,' said Digby.

'But that's stupid. It can't be Fred, it must be
another tortoise.'

'With our phone number
on its back? And a crescent-
shaped mark on the shell,
the lady said.'

They stared at each other.

'But how shall we get
him back?'

'The lady said she was
coming this way this
evening and she'd drop him
off. I gave her our address.'

Just then their mother came in at the garden
gate. 'Have you found where Fred's got to?'
she said.

'Yes,' said Digby.

'Thank goodness for that,' said his mother.
'Otherwise I should have thought there was
something very strange going on. The funniest
thing's just happened. As I was walking up
the lane to the post-box, I saw a bicycle lying

on the grass verge and then a pair of legs sticking out of the ditch. It was old Mr Fosse, you know, the road-mender, and he was lying there as white as a sheet. I helped him out, and you'll never believe the crazy story he told me.'

'What was it?' Dot said.

'He said – he must have been drinking or else he's gone quite potty – he said that he'd been cycling along when suddenly he was

passed by an animal.'

'What sort of animal?' Digby said.

'A tortoise!' his mother said with a shriek of laughter. 'A tortoise, if you please. One really shouldn't laugh at the poor old man. It rushed past him at tremendous speed, and gave him such a shock that he fell off his bike. Talk about seeing pink elephants!'

'Which direction was it going, Mum?' asked Digby.

'Towards Hatch Norton, Mr Fosse said. It was all in the poor old chap's imagination. I mean, imagine Fred dashing past a cyclist. It takes him half a day to cross the lawn.'

At that moment the children heard the distant sound of a car.

'We're going to play out in the lane for a bit, Mum,' Digby said.

Chapter Three

OUTSIDE, THE CHILDREN ran a little way down the lane and stared expectantly at the approaching car. It slowed at the sight of them and then stopped, and a lady wound down the window.

'Are you the children who've lost a tortoise?' she said.

'Yes,' said Digby. 'It's very kind of you to bring him back.'

'Well, I should think you must have given up all hope of seeing him again ages ago,' she said with a smile. 'It must take about a

year for a tortoise to travel two miles!
Sensible of you to have painted your number
on him. Incidentally, how did he get that
funny crescent-shaped mark on his shell?'

'He had an accident,' Digby said quickly.
'Did you touch it? The mark, I mean.'

'No, I certainly did not. I'm sorry, but I'm
afraid I'm not a tortoise lover. They rather
give me the creeps with their snaky heads.
In fact I actually had to put on a pair of
rubber gloves before I could bring myself to
pick him up. Anyway, here he is,' and she
handed a cardboard box out of the car
window.

When they had
thanked her and the
car had driven away
up the lane, Digby
carried the box into
the garden.

'Make sure the
gate's shut this time,
Dot,' he said.

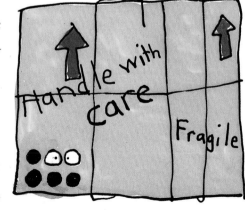

15

In a far corner of the garden, hidden from view, they put the box on the ground and opened it.

'He *looks* just the same as ever,' said Dot.

'Except for that crescent-shaped mark,' said Digby.

'Dig, you're not going to touch it again, are you?'

'Look, I just want to try something,' Digby said. 'D'you think I could lift that big log there with one hand?'

'Don't be silly, Dig, of course you couldn't. It's much too heavy. You couldn't even move it.'

Digby took hold of the log with both hands. He could not budge it an inch.

'You're right,' he said. He took a deep breath, and bending over the box, he pressed his finger to Fred's burn-mark. Then he turned, picked up the log one-handed, and raised it high above his head. Slowly, easily, he lowered it down again.

'Oh!' gasped Dot. 'How could you . . . ? I don't understand.'

'I'm sure it's electricity,' Digby said.

'How do you mean?'

'When that bolt of lightning hit Fred, it must have discharged its electricity into him. That's why he could whizz past old Mr Fosse, and that's why he got to Hatch Norton in ten minutes. Good job that lady did put on her rubber gloves, because Fred's actually become a generator! He's not just Fred any more – he's Lightning Fred! All you've got to do is to touch that mark and Lightning Fred charges your batteries, makes you able to do things that

17

you couldn't possibly do ordinarily, like jump high or lift heavy weights.'

'Or,' said Dot thoughtfully, 'run fast, like he can?'

'Yes!' said Digby. 'Oh, yes, Dot! Of course! Gosh! Are you thinking what I'm thinking?'

'Yes! Sports day. Oh, Dig!'

They stared at each other.

'How long before your . . . your batteries run down again, Dig?'

Digby tried again to lift the log, first with one hand, then with two. He could not budge it.

'Not long, Dot. But long enough.'

Chapter Four

AFTER SUPPER THEY found the cardboard box empty, with a tortoise-shaped hole in one side, slightly charred around its edges.

'Oh, no!' said Dot. 'Now where's Lightning Fred gone?'

'Look!' said Digby, gripping his sister by the arm. 'Look over there!'

Something round and low that seemed to glow in the gathering dusk was rushing across the lawn.

'What a sprinter he'd make!' breathed Digby as the tortoise shot into the shrubbery.

'What a sprinter you'll make, Dig!' said Dot.

First thing next morning, the children found Lightning Fred in the shrubbery, just where he had disappeared at speed the night before. He did not look at all electrified, just the same old Fred, but the old Fred had not had that crescent-shaped burn-mark on his shell.

'After school,' said Digby, 'we'll take him somewhere secret, where no one can see us.'

'And you'll charge your batteries?'

'Yes.'

'And run like the wind!'

'Hope so.'

Before they left home Digby said to his mother, 'You will keep the garden gate shut, won't you?'

'Of course, I always do. Why, specially?'

'Oh, just in case Light . . . just in case Fred should get out.'

His mother laughed. 'He wouldn't get very far if he did get out, would he?'

'Oh, I don't know.'

'Anyway, off you both go to school now or you'll be late. Anything special happening today?'

'There's a practice for the Sports,' Digby said.

The village school was a small one, and there were only nine others of his age in the line-up that afternoon when it came to the time for a trial run of the Boys' Under-Ten 100 metres.

Unfortunately, though Digby's dreams the previous night had all been of racing to victory, he trailed in so far last that the winner had come jogging back past him towards the

start line before he'd even reached the finish.

'Keep going, Dig,' he said as he
passed.

'Good old Dig!' the spectators cried as they
watched his clumsy shambling efforts. Try as
he would, his arms seemed to wave about, his
body to wobble, and his legs, instead of going
straight forward and back like pistons, had
apparently to make a circling movement to
get round his bottom.

Red-faced, puffing, Digby grinned as he
always grinned in defeat. Before, that grin
had been to hide his disappointment,
but now there was another, happier,
reason for it.

TIM   1
Christopher   no 2
Robbie   no 3
David   no 4
Marcus
George
Digby

'Well tried, Digby,' his teacher said, and
to the others, 'we can't all be hares, you
know, and anyway don't forget the fable –
the tortoise won in the end.'

'I'll do better on the day,' Digby said. 'I'm
going into training.' All the boys fell about
laughing.

You just wait, Digby thought.

When school finished, Digby and Dot
hurried home as fast as they could. Would
Lightning Fred have escaped again? Would he
still be supercharged? He hadn't, and he was,
as they could see as soon as they came into
the garden.

The tortoise was grazing on the
lawn, but, startled by the click of
the gate, he took off at top speed,
dashing off like a small runaway
tank to disappear into the
shrubbery. Digby bent over
him.

'You're not going to
charge your batteries yet, are you, Dig?' Dot said.
'Mum might see.'

'No. I just want to make sure that it's only
touching the burn-mark that does it and that
anywhere else is O.K. After all, we're going to
have to carry him around with us. On Sports

Day you'll have to carry him.'

'Oh, no!'

'It'll be all right, Dot, I'm certain. Look, I'll try and then you can.'

Digby reached down and scratched the top of Lightning Fred's head, then his leathery old neck, then, in turn, each leg, and finally he put his hand on the shell, the front of it, the back, the sides, everywhere except the crescent-shaped mark.

'There, you see, I didn't feel anything. It's only that one place. Go on, you try now, Dot.'

'Oh, Dig, must I?'

'Yes.'

Gingerly, making a dreadful face, Dot began to copy what her brother had done.

'See, I told you it's all right. Pick him up.'

'Oh, no! Suppose he runs away with me?'

'He can't run if his feet are off the ground. Go on, Dot, you've got to. Otherwise the plan won't work.'

'I can't. I'm frightened.'

Digby played his trump card. 'Oh, all right then. If you can't help me I shall just trail in last in the race. As usual.'

The thought of this was too much for Dot. Biting her lip, she grasped Lightning Fred with both hands, one on each side of his shell, and lifted him up.

'I did it!' she said. The tortoise stared owlishly at her.

'Come on,' said Digby. 'We'll go up the lane to that long narrow field by the wood. I'll carry him.'

When they reached the field, Digby gave the tortoise carefully back to Dot and marked out a rough 100 metres with two sticks, counting aloud and taking large clumsy steps.

'If only he can win that race!' said Dot softly to

Lightning Fred. 'It's got to work. It must work.'

Once Digby had measured out his track, he came back to the starting stick. They stared at each other.

'Good luck, Dig,' said Dot.

Digby looked round but the only other living thing to be seen was an old horse peering over a gate at the far end.

'Right. Here goes,' he said.

He turned to face the finish.

'Hold him out, Dot,' he said,

and when she obeyed he put a finger firmly on the crescent-shaped burn-mark.

Watching him intently, Dot saw a shiver run through him. Then after a little pause, so suddenly that it made her jump, Digby was off, tearing along the field faster than she had ever seen any boy run, faster than any boy ever *had* run. There was no change in his style – his arms still waved wildly about, his body still wobbled, his legs still swung around his fat bottom – but everything waved or wobbled or swung five times as fast as usual. It was like a speeded-up film.

Almost before Dot could draw breath, Digby was passing the finishing stick, travelling at such speed that he only just managed to pull up before the far hedge. Horrified, the old

horse galloped away. Digby turned and began
to walk back, punching both fists in the air
with excitement.

'Dig! Dig!' yelled Dot. 'Try running back. See

if it's still working.'

'All right!' shouted Digby, but when he set off again, it was at the old plodding pace.

'It doesn't last long,' he panted when he reached his sister.

'But long enough! Gosh, you were *flying* along, Dig. I don't know how you kept your balance.'

'It was so easy,' said Digby. 'I just felt as light as a feather, and yet so strong! It was marvellous!'

'Are you going to have another go?'

'No. I'd love to but I don't think I'd better. We know it works for running now, and for long enough for me to win the 100 metres. But what we don't know is how long I can go on recharging from Lightning Fred without using up his power. We must save it for Sports Day.'

Chapter Five

ON THE MORNING of Sports Day, Dot carried her shoe bag to school. She had left her trainers and P.E. kit in her locker, and the bag, which she hung up in the changing room, contained only Lightning Fred. Somehow the morning, and lunch (Digby could hardly eat a thing) seemed to drag by, but at last the moment came.

The infants had had their little races, the long jumpers and the high jumpers had

performed, and Dot's part in the Sports was over. She had come fourth out of seven in the Girls' Under-Eight 70 metres, of which she was quite proud, considering the shortness of her legs.

Now she asked her teacher, 'Can I go to the toilet, please?'

Once indoors she quickly took the shoe bag from its hook, opened it, checked the tortoise, and popped a clean handkerchief inside.

Everyone was watching the girls of Digby's age racing, and Dot made her way carefully to the starting-line and stood near to one end of it. Within a few minutes the call came, 'Boys' Under-Ten 100 metres!' and the ten competitors began to line up, Digby making sure he was closest to his sister.

'Are you ready?' called the teacher who was starting the races.

'Just a minute, sir,' said Digby quickly. 'Can I blow my nose?'

'It's supposed to be you that's running, Digby – not your nose.'

'Oh, please, my sister's got a hanky.'

'Hurry up, then.'

Quickly, Dot pushed the shoe bag towards him, its mouth open. Quickly he pretended to use the handkerchief while with the first finger of his other hand he found and pressed the magic mark. Then he was back in the line-up, tensed, quivering, ready.

'One . . . Two . . . Three . . .' but at 'Three' several of the keenest made a false start.

'Come back!' called the teacher. 'Come on back, you lot.'

The seconds ticked by, as the offenders trailed back, maddeningly slowly.

'Dig! Dig!' hissed Dot through the noise of the spectators. 'It'll be too late!'

They stared at each other.

'Sir!' cried Digby desperately. 'I need to blow my nose again!'

'Don't be silly, Digby, I can't wait for you and your nose. Now then, One . . . Two . . . Three . . . GO!'

To the watchers it seemed that Digby was

still fumbling about for his handkerchief as
the other nine sped away. They had covered
twenty metres before he took his hand from
the shoe bag again, but the shouts of glee that
arose at the sight of old Digby – of all the
people – still fiddling about when the race
had started were suddenly stilled as he shot
off in pursuit. Only Dot's shout of 'Come on,
Dig!' broke the awestruck silence.

At thirty metres he had cut
their lead to half,

at forty he was level,

at fifty well ahead, and from then on all
that the other runners saw was a

disappearing blur of arms and legs as he
hurtled away from them like a greyhound

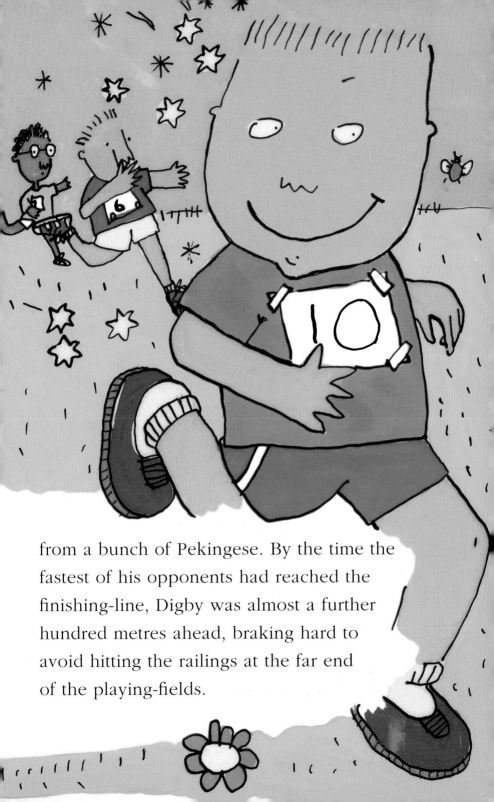

from a bunch of Pekingese. By the time the
fastest of his opponents had reached the
finishing-line, Digby was almost a further
hundred metres ahead, braking hard to
avoid hitting the railings at the far end
of the playing-fields.

Then he turned and walked slowly, clumsily, back to the rest of the school, the  remains of the burst finishing-tape wrapped around his proudly heaving chest, the usual grin on his red face. How they cheered!

Later, Digby just couldn't recall the rest of that Sports Day. Still to come were all the events for the oldest children – their running races, the obstacle race, the egg-and-spoon, the Marathon (twice round the playing-fields) – but all he could remember afterwards was the look of amazement on the face of the headmaster as, amidst a storm of applause, he presented him with the cup for the Boys' Under-Ten 100 metres.

'Well done, Digby!' he said. 'I don't know what got into you!'

'It was quite a shock, sir,' Digby said.

When they reached home (Dot was allowed to hold the little cup, while Digby carried the shoe bag), they put Lightning Fred out on the lawn, and dashed indoors.

'Mum! Mum!' yelled Dot. 'Dig won his race!' and she showed her the trophy.

'Digby!' cried his mother. 'How super! I didn't know you were a fast runner.' She gave him a hug. 'To be truthful,' she said, smiling, 'I didn't think you were much faster than old Fred!'

Digby smiled too. 'I'm not,' he said.

They all looked out of the window and there on the grass stood the tortoise, motionless at the spot where the children had placed him. And as they watched, they saw

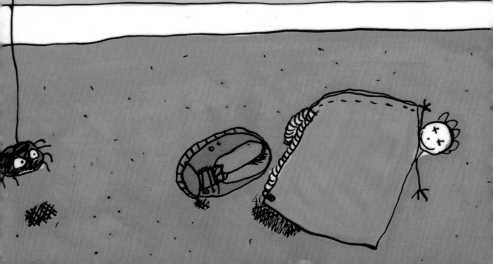

him, very cautiously, stick out his snaky old head, and then, very very slowly, reach out first with one foot and then another, and start to crawl at a snail's pace across the lawn.

'At least I wasn't,' said Digby. 'Even today.'

'But now it looks as if you are again,' said Dot.

They stared at each other.

Then they suddenly burst out laughing.

42

Yellow Bananas are bright, funny, brilliantly imaginative stories written by some of today's top writers. All the books are beautifully illustrated in full colour.

So if you've enjoyed this story, why not pick another one from the bunch?